Litt

Peter's

Surprise Goods

by

Christopher Vine

The watercolour illustrations are by John Wardle

Published by
Christopher Vine 2011
Reprinted 2015

Printed by The Amadeus Press

ISBN 978-0-9553359-69

RY FOX

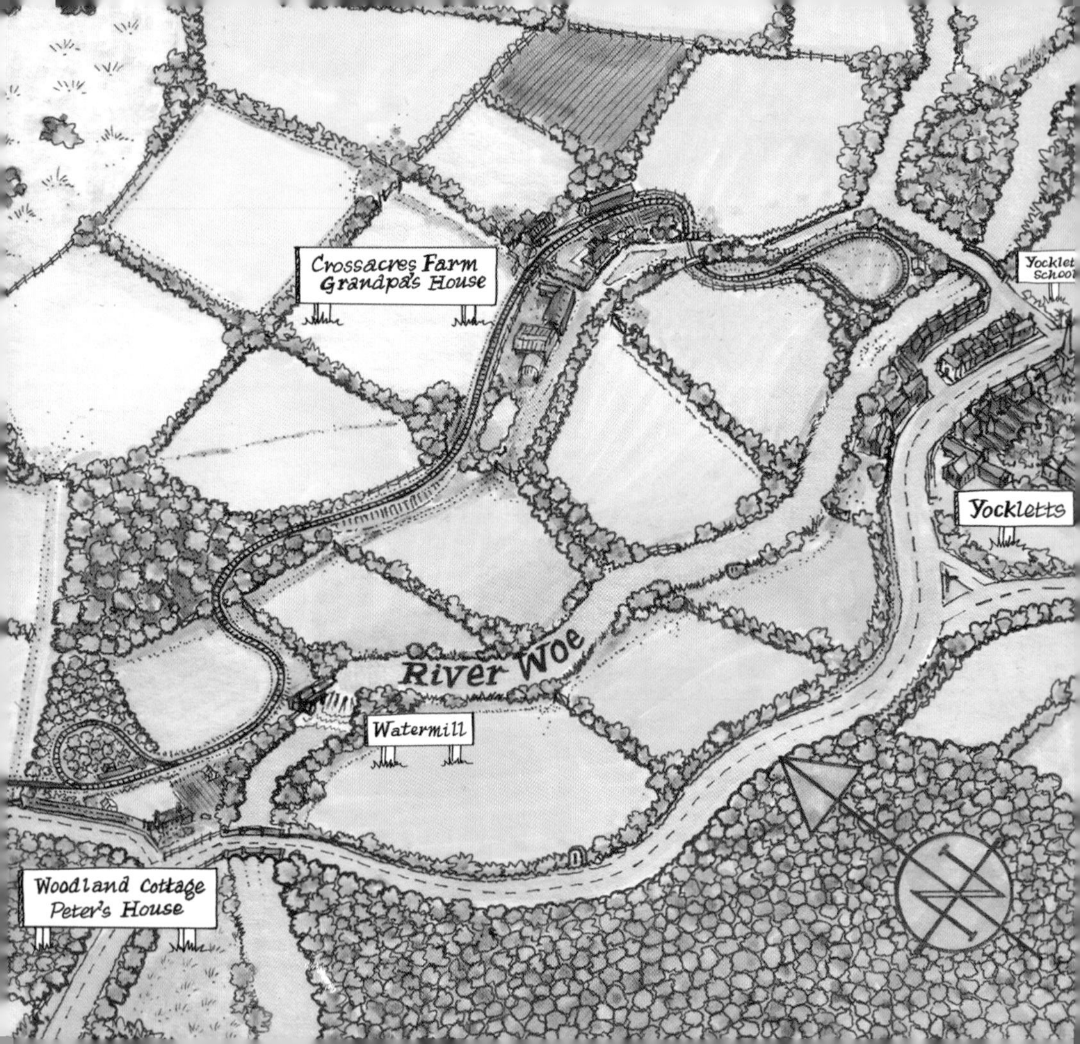
Crossacres Farm
Grandpa's House
Yocklet
Schoo
Yockletts
River Woe
Watermill
Woodland Cottage
Peter's House

The Peter's Railway Series

Peter and his Grandpa have built an amazing miniature steam railway between their houses, Woodland Cottage and Crossacres Farm. The line even runs to Yockletts Village where Peter goes to school.

The locomotive, Fiery Fox, is a wonderful machine. Bright green and very powerful.

Grandpa and Peter have spent countless happy hours building the railway and working on their other projects. They have had many adventures along the way.

Peter's little sister and brother, Kitty and Harry, are now getting old enough to enjoy the railway too. This is a story about them.

Surprise Goods

It was a busy day at Crossacres Farm and the young twins, Kitty and Harry, were very excited. Today was their birthday.

Peter and Grandpa had organised a special railway party for them and their friends.

Grandma produced one of her slap up teas which they had on the train as it sped along. They ate jam sandwiches as they cruised past the duck pond, biscuits on the way through the woods and drank milk shakes as they crossed a large field of Highland cows. How appropriate!

At Yewston station, Kitty and Harry blew out the candles on their cake and then everyone went on a treasure hunt round the garden.

P.R.

The best bit of the afternoon had been when they helped Peter to drive the train.

They had taken turns to ride on Fiery Fox, sitting at the front of the tender. Reaching into the cab, they could blow the steam whistle by pulling a lever.

They had to give a loud "Toot Toot" to warn the cows and sheep that the train was approaching.

They blew the whistle much more often than was necessary, but that made it even more fun!

"If you keep blowing that whistle," Peter had joked, "we won't have any steam left to pull the train! I'll put some more coal on the fire to keep us going."

Now it was evening and time to settle down with Mum for a bed-time story. "What kind of story would you like?" she asked them.

"A story about trains!" they both shouted together, bouncing up and down on the sofa.

"But I'm not very good at telling train stories," said Mum quietly. "How about a nice story about elephants, mermaids and..."

"No! A train story!" they both chanted, still bouncing up and down in a most un-sleepy sort of way.

"Alright, I'll do my best," said Mum. "But remember: it won't be like the stories your Grandpa tells..."

Peter's Railway
and the Moonlight Express
Christopher Vine

"Once upon a time," began Mum, "there was an extra special goods train with a top secret load.

"It had twenty five loaded wagons and was hauled by a modern and very powerful electric locomotive.

"Even with such a long and heavy train, the electric engine pulled it easily and was speeding through the night.

"Mr Faraday, the driver, was wide awake, as he had had a good sleep during the day. He loved his job and was enjoying every minute of the journey.

"The stars were out and there was a full moon to light up the countryside as the train headed north."

All of a sudden, the electric locomotive lost power and started to slow down. Soon it ground to a halt in the middle of nowhere. There had been a power cut and, without electricity, the train was stuck!

Mr Faraday picked up the telephone in his cab and called the nearest signal box to ask for assistance.

"Don't worry," the signalman told him. "We will send out a diesel engine to rescue you. Just wait where you are and it will be along soon."

A little while later, a rather old and smoky diesel engine arrived, driven by Mr Otto. He coupled on to the train and Mr Faraday climbed into his cab to ride with him.

They set off into the night with a huge roar.

Mile after mile they powered along the track, hauling the electric engine and the heavy train.

Suddenly some red warning lamps lit up in Mr Otto's cab, followed soon after by a loud banging noise from behind. "Oh dear!" he shouted above the din. "I shall have to shut the engine down, there's something terribly wrong!"

Once again the heavy train came to a stop.

Mr Otto and Mr Faraday went through a small door in the rear of the cab, and into the power compartment. They tried to fix the damaged engine but the fault was too serious and they had to give up. Something deep inside the machine had gone wrong.

Now it was Mr Otto's turn to call the signal box and ask for help.

"I'm very sorry," came the reply, "but we don't have any more spare engines. You will just have to wait until morning. Goodbye."

"But my top secret load," exclaimed Mr Faraday. "I must deliver it on time!"

"I know what to do," said Mr Otto. "We are only a few miles south of York and the wonderful National Railway Museum. The Chief Engineer is a good friend, I'll call him and ask if they have a locomotive that could help."

Mr Gibbon was working late in the workshop when the phone rang... "Yes, of course we will help you, Mr Otto," he answered. "We have an engine which is still hot from running this afternoon. We'll stoke up the fire and be out in half an hour. Wait there!"

While Mr Faraday and Mr Otto settled down to wait in the cab of the broken diesel engine, there was a hive of activity at the museum.

Mr Gibbon and his assistant climbed up into the cab of the old steam locomotive and set to work.

There were only a few glowing embers left in the fire so they shovelled more coal on. Soon the flames were heating the boiler and the old girl started sizzling quietly to herself. The pressure was rising.

They oiled all her beautiful old machinery and checked there was plenty of water in the tender. It wouldn't do to run out!

At last they were ready.

The two men pushed open the heavy shed doors and climbed back up to the cab.

Mallard was a fabulous engine. She had been built in 1938 and to this very day (or night), still holds the official speed record for the fastest steam locomotive in the world.

Of course, she was designed to pull express passenger trains, not broken down goods trains. But Mr Gibbon had every confidence in his old engine; this was going to be quite an adventure.

Slowly they steamed out of the shed, past some green signals, over some points and out onto the main line.

Then they stopped and reversed for a few miles to reach the stricken train.

Nº 4468

They slowed down when they saw it and stopped just as the buffers clanged together.

"Are we pleased to see you!" shouted up Mr Faraday and Mr Otto. "We'll couple you on in half a jiffy."

Then they climbed the steps into the cosy warm cab of the old steam engine: They wouldn't miss a ride on Mallard for anything. "Third time lucky!" shouted Mr Otto.

"I don't think we'll need luck," chuckled Mr Gibbon. "This is a reliable old engine. No need for other people's electricity and no parts hidden away where I can't see or mend them!"

Mr Gibbon opened the regulator and, with a few wheezes and clouds of steam, they were off.

Mallard was superb. No one would have guessed that she was nearly a hundred years old.

Mr Gibbon was enjoying himself too. It wasn't often he got the chance to take her out on the main line, especially for a long run like this.

More coal on the fire, more water in the boiler. Mallard charged through the night like a race horse, the miles disappearing under her wheels.

All too soon they reached their destination and, slowing down, they pulled into a large goods yard. Mallard, the two broken down engines and the top secret load had arrived.

When they pulled up at the buffers, Mr Faraday opened the wagons to help unload them.

"What was in them?" asked Harry excitedly. "Was it gold?"

Mum shook her head. "No, try again."

"Was it diamonds?" guessed Kitty. "Or maybe it was secret inventions?"

"No," replied Mum, giggling. "Every wagon was packed full to bursting with goodnight hugs, kisses and cuddles!"

"Oh Mum!" the twins groaned.

"And I've got them all here, just for you two!" she laughed, scooping them both up in her arms. "Time for bed!"

Good night and happy dreams...

The End.

Why Peter's Railway?

Since a very small boy, Chris has always loved everything mechanical, especially steam engines. The first workshop was in his bedroom where he made an electric go-kart when only 8, followed by a mini-bike powered by the engine from a petrol lawn mower.

He spent many holidays on a friend's farm where there was a miniature railway across a field and so started a love of making model steam locomotives. The latest is Bongo, 8 feet long and the inspiration for Fiery Fox in the books.

Chris wanted to share his love and knowledge of railways and engineering: Peter's Railway is the result.

Books for children who love trains and engineering

Story

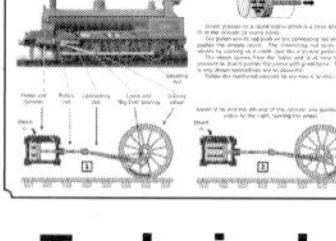

Technical

History

Adventure

The hardback books

The five hardback books tell the charming story of Peter and his Grandpa building and running their steam railway across the farm. At the ends of chapters are special how-it-works pages with simple (but accurate) explanations of what has been happening in the story. In addition, Grandpa tells some wonderful stories from the old days on the railways. Age range 6 - 12 years approx.

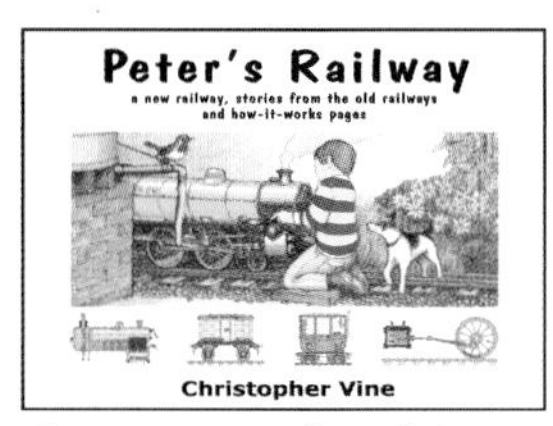

A new steam railway is born.

Points, turntables and Peter drives Fiery Fox.

The line is extended and The Great Railway Race.

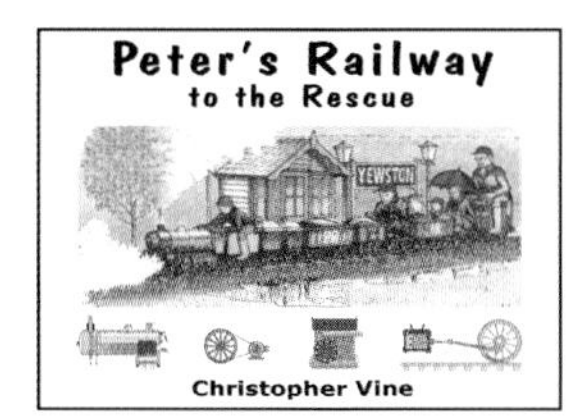

They build a watermill to power the farm.

Peter helps save the world and makes lots of money!

Activity book with puzzles and colouring. Paperback.

Hardback, 96 pages 17 x 24 cm with 30 watercolour pictures by John Wardle and 14 pages of clearly explained technical drawings. £11.99

Paperback books

A series of Peter's Railway in a smaller format. While the original books each contain several story or adventure threads, separate technical pages and Grandpa's tales, the small books concentrate on one aspect; an adventure, a tale from the old railways or a technical book. Age 6 - 12 years approx.

An adventure on a Scottish holiday ends with a bang!	A true story about an unlucky locomotive.	A dramatic true story from the old days.	A cab-ride in a modern train and a tale of disaster.	Our two heroes make a new engine from scrap.	Grandpa answers a tricky question.

"Little" Peter's Railway are gentle stories for younger children. Age 3 - 6 years approx.

The children foil a plot and cause destruction!

Peter saves Christmas, a gentle tale.	A bed-time story with a twist.	A railway picnic soon turns into mayhem...